Albert's World Tour

Albert the Dragon's adopted children, the Dragonettes, are growing noisier and more boisterous every
day. Albert, as good-natured as ever, would be the
last to admit that being a parent is getting him
down, but he is delighted when his old friend Tony
suggests a holiday.

Together, Tony and Albert plan a trip round the
world, with a visit to Africa to see the lions, and to
China, where the people like dragons.

Albert has doubts about foreign travel, but he
pushes them aside and takes off, with Tony as
passenger, south towards France and beyond. It is
an eventful trip, full of surprises, pleasant and
unpleasant . . .

Albert's World Tour

Rosemary Weir

Illustrated by David McKee

A Grasshopper Book

Abelard · London

ISBN 0 200 72570 X (hardback)
ISBN 0 200 72571 8 (paperback)

Abelard-Schuman Limited
A member of the Blackie Group
450 Edgware Road
London W2 1EG

Printed in Great Britain by
Thomson Litho Ltd, East Kilbride, Scotland

Tony has an Idea

Albert the Dragon came out of his cave on to the little beach which he called his own, blinked in the warm sunshine and stretched out lazily on the hot sand. Not far off the Dragonettes, Alberto and Albertina, were paddling happily in a rock pool, the sun glinting off their blue and green scales. Albert regarded them fondly.

"The dear little things," he murmured to himself. "It seems only yesterday that I found those two eggs abandoned on my doorstep, and now here they are, safely hatched and growing like mad. What a lucky chap I am!"

With a contented sigh he dropped off to sleep.

He was awakened a few minutes later by Alberto shouting in his ear.

"Uncle Albert! Uncle Albert! What *do* you think?"

"I wasn't thinking at all," said Albert mildly. "I was just having forty winks. Whatever is the matter, Berto? Has something upset you? You've got smoke coming out of your nose."

"I'm getting hot," said Berto proudly. "All dragons get hot when they're angry, don't they, Uncle Albert? I'm *awfully* angry!"

Albertina raced across the beach and plopped down at Albert's side.

"Uncle Albert!" she said. "What *do* you think?"

"I've asked him that already," Berto told her. "Look, Tina, I'm getting hot. See my scales turning red? That's because I'm angry. I'll bet you can't turn your scales red. Girls can't."

"Of course they can," said Albert quickly. "Don't tease your sister, Berto. She could get hot and angry just as well as you can, but she isn't going to, are you, my little pet?"

"I don't see why I shouldn't if Berto does," said Tina. "He always thinks he can do things better because he's a boy. It's not fair."

"Suppose you both tell me what you're angry about?" suggested Albert. "Then we can decide whether it's worth getting all hot and bothered."

"If we decide it is, will you get hot too?" demanded Berto. "Will you turn red all over and blow smoke and flames out of your nose?"

"We'll see," Albert said cautiously. It was a very warm day and he really didn't want to go through all that performance. It was ages since anything had made him angry enough to blow flames out of his nose and he knew he was out of practice. "You still haven't told me what's upsetting you both."

"There's someone living in our old cave up on the cliff top," shouted Berto.

"It's a fox," said Tina.

"'Tisn't," said Berto. "It's a badger."

"Badgers don't live in caves," said Tina scornfully. "If it isn't a fox it's a unicorn."

Berto yelled with laughter.

"A unicorn!" he spluttered. "Did you hear her, Uncle Albert? A unicorn! Anyone knows there's no such thing as a unicorn! It's a fab—fab—what-

8

d'you-call-it monster."

"Fabulous is the word you want," said Albert. "Only it isn't. I met a unicorn once, a charming fellow, in great distress—I was able to give him a little help."

"Well, it isn't a unicorn in the old cave anyway," said Berto. "I bet you fifty cowrie shells it isn't."

"You mustn't bet," said Albert. "It's a bad habit. Why are you so angry at the idea of anyone living in our old cave? We don't need it any more."

"*Well*," said Berto. "It's such cheek. They might have asked first."

"They wouldn't know who to ask," said Albert. "It's a whole year since we moved out and they may be newcomers to the district."

"Here comes Tony," said Tina, looking across the sands. "He'll know who it is. Hi, Tony!"

"Hi, you two," said Tony, plopping down beside Albert and fanning himself with his hat. "Hi, Albert. Whew, I'm boiling! I've been helping Dad get in the hay."

"Tony, my dear old friend," said Albert. "How very nice to see you. Perhaps you can settle an argument. The children tell me there is someone living in our old cave. Tina says it's a fox and Berto is quite sure it's a badger. There is also some talk of it being a unicorn. Can you throw any light on the matter?"

"Wrong every time," said Tony. He chuckled. "A unicorn! I must tell Mary Ann that when she arrives tomorrow. It'll make her laugh. All the same what's in the cave is more like a unicorn than a badger."

"Told you so!" said Tina, nudging her brother.

9

"It's an old billy goat," said Tony. "I don't know where he came from, but he's been wandering about on the moors for some time, living rough. I told him he could use the cave if he liked because he was complaining about the damp. You don't mind, do you, Albert?"

"Not in the least, my dear fellow," said Albert. "I make no claim to the old cave. When you and the children were clever enough to find these splendid new quarters for us all, and brave enough to evict that dreadful sea-serpent, I should be ungrateful indeed to hanker after the old cave."

"That's all right then," said Tony and Albert said, "Did I understand you to say that dear Mary Ann was coming to the farm tomorrow?"

"That's right. She's coming to stay for several months. Mother needs a helping hand and Mary Ann can be spared from her own home now because the next eldest girl, Sukie, is big enough to take her place and help with the younger children."

"We must have a party to welcome her," said Albert excitedly. "Berto, Tina, why don't you go and catch some shrimps? Mary Ann is very fond of a shrimp tea."

"Bet I catch more shrimps than Tina!" shouted Berto. Tina burst into tears.

"He won't, will he, Uncle Albert?" she sobbed.

"Oh my goodness!" said Albert. "How do I know? Dry your eyes, get your shrimping net and see what you can do."

The Dragonettes stumped off across the beach to the rock pools, arguing all the way. Albert sighed, and plopped back on to the sand.

"Those kids are getting you down," said Tony

sympathetically.

"Not at all," said Albert. "Never think that, Tony, please. It's just that they do quarrel rather a lot, and Tina cries too easily. Now Berto has learned how to breathe smoke and fire I'm afraid there will be more trouble. He'd really worked himself up about a stranger living in our cave, the silly boy."

"You need a holiday from them," said Tony firmly. "You ought to take a holiday, Albert."

"A holiday?" repeated Albert. "Remember the holiday we took together, all those years ago? What fun we had. Ah, happy days."

"Why don't we do it again?" suggested Tony. "Dad says I can have some time off when all the hay is in and before harvest time. Oh Albert, do let's!"

Albert's eyes sparkled.

"You'd come with me?" he exclaimed. "That would be wonderful!" Then his face clouded. "How can I?" he said sadly. "The Dragonettes—"

"Mary Ann would look after them," said Tony. "She could sleep down here if we put a bed in the cave, and go up to the farm part of each day to help Mother. She'd love it, and you know how good she is with children."

"You really think she would?" said Albert. "It's asking a great deal."

"I know she would!" said Tony confidently. "Albert, can you still fly?"

"Of course I can," said Albert indignantly. "I may be a tiny bit out of practice, but it would soon come back to me. I'd take *you* anywhere you want to go, my young friend."

"Right!" said Tony, jumping to his feet. "Then take me round the world!"

Mr MacSporran

Albert stared at Tony in amazement.

"Round the *world*?" he repeated. "*Round* the world? Tony did I hear you correctly?"

"Yes. Why not?" said Tony calmly. "It's quite easy. You only have to turn to the south and keep on flying and in time you come back to where you started."

"Are you sure?" said Albert and Tony nodded. "Positive," he said. "I learnt it in school."

Albert thought for a moment.

"What happens if you turn to the north?" he said at last.

"Same thing only the other way round. But it's best to turn south from here because that way you cross the channel and get to France."

"You astound me," said Albert. "How long would it take?"

"Not long," Tony told him carelessly. "You fly pretty fast, and we wouldn't want to spend too long in foreign parts. Just a quick look at—er— China, and a day or two in Darkest Africa to see the lions— "

"Lions!" exclaimed Albert. "I'm not sure I like the sound of that!"

"Good gracious me, you've no need to be afraid of lions," Tony said. "You're much, much bigger than any lion."

"Possibly," said Albert, thinking hard. "And what is China?"

"You mean *where* is China," Tony corrected him. "It's—it's—well it's round the other side, I think. I should know it when I saw it. They are very fond of dragons in China."

"Are they really?" said Albert. "What a lot you know, Tony. What else do they have?"

"Lots of things," said Tony. "They have little tiny dogs that live up people's sleeves."

"Why do they do that?" asked Albert.

"*I* don't know. I suppose they like it. We might bring one back for the Dragonettes."

"Yes!" said Albert, quite entering into the spirit of the thing. "Or we might bring them a lion, a very small one!"

"You'll come then?" asked Tony. Albert looked solemn.

"I'll think it over," he promised. "It doesn't do to rush into these things. First we must find out if Mary Ann is willing to look after Berto and Tina."

"She'll be willing," said Tony confidently, and sure enough, Mary Ann agreed at once. She came down alone to the cave late on the evening she arrived at the farm and sat on a rock watching the sun set over the bay.

"It's lovely here," she said. "There's nothing I would like better than staying in the cave for a week or two. I met that elderly goat who's living in your old home now and he was saying how much he enjoys the sunsets."

"I haven't had the pleasure of meeting him yet," said Albert. "What is he like?"

14

"He's very interesting," said Mary Ann. "He's travelled a lot and he's full of stories about his adventures in foreign parts."

"Tony and I will be full of stories when we come back," said Albert rather jealously, and Mary Ann said quickly, "I know you will. Where are you going first, Albert?"

Albert looked confused. He really knew nothing about geography at all and had never been further from home than the Scilly Isles which are just off the end of Cornwall so he didn't know what to say. Luckily just at that moment the Dragonettes came rushing across the beach, full of excitement at seeing their dear Mary Ann, and then Tony arrived, so Albert was able to lean across to him and say:

"Tony, old chap, what was that place we decided to visit?"

"China," said Tony.

"China! That's it. Where the little dogs are," said Albert.

"It's an awfully long way," said Mary Ann, doubtfully.

"Albert will make nothing of it," said Tony. "Anyway, we may break the journey on a desert island. I was talking to that goat—"

"Everyone seems to have met him except me," exclaimed Albert.

"Well, you don't go out much, do you?" reasoned Tony. "You could meet him if you wanted to. He's very interesting. He's travelled all over the world."

"We've invited him to supper tonight!" burst in Tina excitedly. "You don't mind, do you, Uncle Albert?"

"You'd better all stay," said Albert. "Let's make

15

a party of it. There won't be much to eat I'm afraid unless—er—Mary Ann—?"

"I'll go and fetch a basket," laughed Mary Ann, and Tony said, "I'll catch some fish. You kids can collect seaweed."

"What do goats like best?" asked Berto, and Mary Ann said, "Leave that to me. I'll ask Uncle to let me have a bundle of hay and some crushed oats."

Promptly at six o'clock the goat arrived. He was very large and shaggy with spreading horns and a pointed beard. He introduced himself as Daniel MacSporran and seemed so very much a man of the world that simple old Albert felt quite shy. It seemed that the stranger had been for many years the mascot of one of the Highland regiments which explained his world-wide travels. He had just retired and come to live in Cornwall because of the soft air and also because he had a sister living in the neighbourhood. When it turned out that this sister was the very goat called Bella who had helped Albert during his troublesome time with the baby centaur they felt as if they had known each other for years.

After supper, as they all sat in a circle outside the cave in the light of a full moon, Albert said:

"Mr MacSporran, Tony and I are planning a little trip around the world, by air, of course. Could you give us a few tips on where to go and what to see? I must confess I'm just a little nervous, never having been further than the Isles of Scilly in my life."

"There's nothing to it, my dear chap," said the goat. "And do call me Dan. Don't treat me like a stranger."

"I'm a bit worried about making myself understood in foreign parts—er—Dan," said Albert.

"Don't be," said Dan. "Most foreigners can understand English if they try. Just speak a bit louder, that's all."

"It sounds very simple," said Albert doubtfully.

"It is," said Dan. "If anyone pretended not to understand me I used to butt them with my horns. It always worked wonders."

"But I haven't any horns," objected Albert. "And it sounds rather unkind."

"Nothing of the sort. They like it," said Dan.

Albert was silent. He had always found goats a bit queer and Dan seemed queerer than most. Tony saved the situation by asking how far Dan reckoned it was to China and how long the flight would take.

"Difficult to say, my dear boy," said Dan. "If

17

you're flying, two or three days at the most. I went there by troop ship which took longer of course, but was very comfortable. I always had V.I.P. treatment, you know. I suppose you could say I was the most important person in the regiment. I had my own soldier servant and you should have seen the coats I wore on parade."

"Did you bring the soldiers good luck?" asked Tina shyly.

"Of course I did, my dear," said Dan. "That's what mascots are for."

It was very late when Daniel MacSporran left and went home to the cliff top cave. Tina and Berto were yawning their heads off, while Mary Ann and Tony had left some time before, saying they had to be up early for the milking. Tony winked at Albert as he said good-night and murmured, "What a conceited old bore!" Albert quite agreed with him but was too polite to show the slightest sign of wanting his guest to go home.

"And he didn't even tell us anything useful," he thought to himself as he followed the sleepy Dragonettes into the cave. "Oh well, I've no doubt Tony and I will manage very well on our own."

The Tour Begins

It was decided that The Great Trip should start on June 21st which left just under a week to prepare. Albert had never been so busy in his life. It wasn't that he actually had much to do, but he did everything several times over before he was absolutely certain it was right. He tidied the cave so thoroughly that neither he nor the Dragonettes could find any of their things, he collected a great pile of seaweed to take with him and then threw it away and collected more, because seaweed, once out of the sea, soon goes dry and smells horrid. Mary Ann made him two pannier bags fastened together with a strap which he could wear over his back and these he packed and repacked at least three times a day.

"Leave one for me," Tony said when he came down to the cave to see how Albert was getting on. "I'll have to take a change of clothes in case it rains. What are you packing, anyway?"

Albert looked confused. "Just this and that," he said shyly.

"He's packing seaweed and little bushes!" shouted Berto. "He keeps putting them in and taking them out."

"*Food*?" said Tony. "No need for that, Albert. We'll find plenty to eat on the way."

"But what about if we come down in the desert?" said Albert, his forehead all wrinkled with worry.

"We won't," said Tony. "Oh, Albert, do stop fussing and leave it all to me. I've learnt geography at school and I know the way."

With this Albert had to be content, but he sneaked just a little seaweed and a few very small branches from a juniper bush into the bottom of one of the bags and hoped no one would notice.

"It's always as well to be prepared," he murmured to himself.

The twenty-first of June was a lovely day, clear, warm and sunny. Tony and Mary Ann came down to the cave at first light and they all had a picnic breakfast on the beach. The Dragonettes were looking rather solemn and Tina had tears in her eyes, but Mary Ann took a claw of each and held them in her warm clasp while Tony climbed up on to Albert's back, took a firm hold of the band—also made by Mary Ann—around his neck, and said, "Off we go!"

"Goodbye Berto, goodbye Tina, be good," said Albert in rather a choked voice. "Goodbye Mary Ann. We'll be back almost before you know we've gone."

"We jolly well won't," said Tony. "Dad's given me a month's holiday and we're not coming back a day before it's up. Come on, Albert, get going!"

Albert took a little run, flapped his wings and rose slowly and ponderously into the air. He circled round Mary Ann and the Dragonettes a couple of times gaining height until they looked like little black specks against the sand and then they were off, sailing through the clear blue sky.

"Turn left!" Tony yelled in his ear. "Don't you know your left from your right?"

"Of course I do," said Albert, turning round so hastily that Tony nearly fell off. "I was only admiring the sunrise."

"Never mind the sunrise, just head for Europe," shouted Tony. "We ought to get as far as Rome by tonight."

"Anything interesting to see in Rome?" asked Albert. He was flying steadily now and could give his mind to other things.

"Lots of buildings I believe," said Tony. "It's a very old place. The people who live there are called

21

Romans."

"Only what you'd expect," said Albert wisely, and after that there was no more talk until they had crossed the English Channel and saw the coast of France.

"I'm beginning to feel a bit hungry," said Albert suddenly. "Shall we go down and see what we can find for lunch?"

"People in France eat frogs," said Tony doubtfully. "Do you fancy frogs, Albert?"

"My dear Tony, you know very well that I am a vegetarian. Besides I *like* frogs, just as friends. Surely there must be other things to eat in France?"

"Let's go down and see," suggested Tony and Albert landed gently and carefully in a green field by the side of a crystal clear stream. Bushes of a kind well known to Albert grew in profusion and it was all so like Cornwall that he felt quite at home.

"If this is foreign parts I like it very much," he said happily. "I can make a good lunch here."

"It's all very well for you," said Tony. "But what about me? I'm so hungry I could even eat frogs."

"My dear old friend, how could I be so selfish?" exclaimed Albert. He looked around and started violently as he saw something large and white moving behind a small clump of trees.

"Someone's coming!" he whispered. "It's—why, I really believe I know who it is. It's the Unicorn!"

Out from the shelter of the trees stepped a beautiful horse-like creature with a gilded horn in the middle of his forehead. His pure white coat gleamed in the sunlight and his mild eyes looked at Albert and Tony with a nervousness which suddenly changed to pleasure as he bounded forward crying,

"Albert! My dear old friend!"

"We met some years ago in Cornwall," Albert explained to Tony and turned to greet the Unicorn with little puffs of excited smoke coming through his nose.

"But what are you doing here?" asked the Unicorn when the first greetings were over.

"We're on a World Tour," said Albert proudly. "This is our first stop. We thought of lunching here but although I am well provided for my poor Tony can find nothing he cares to eat."

"Have you forgotten that I can grant wishes?" said the Unicorn. He turned to Tony. "What do you fancy? No, don't tell me. Just think it, and I'll do the rest."

Tony shut his eyes, the better to think, and the Unicorn stood looking at him kindly. Then he stamped a hoof, shook his head and said, "Open your eyes."

Tony did as he was told and gave a yell of surprise. On the green turf in front of him stood a table with a chair drawn up to it all ready for him to start his meal. On the table was a cold chicken with a beautiful salad, a large dish of strawberry ice cream and a basket of the most delicious fruit.

"I didn't think of the fruit," stammered Tony.

"No, that was my own idea," said the Unicorn. "I just thought you might fancy it, and Albert too, seeing that he's a vegetarian."

"I can't think how you do it," said Albert admiringly, and the Unicorn smiled modestly and said, "It's all in the mind."

It was a wonderful lunch. Tony sat down at the table and tucked in while Albert and the Unicorn

wandered about taking a bite here and a bite there and they all ended up by drinking the sparkling cold water of the stream.

"But you haven't told me yet what you are doing here?" enquired Albert and the Unicorn said, "It's quite simple. I live here."

"Then you're French?" said Tony. "But you speak English?"

"I speak anything that's needed. Yes, I am French and proud of it. I have a beautiful French wife and two beautiful French children. Would you like to meet them?"

"Very much," said Albert. "But we mustn't be too long. You see we are on our way round the world."

"I live quite close," said the Unicorn. "Just over the hill and—" He stopped suddenly as a terrible scream of fright came tearing through the stillness of the summer day.

A Muddle with Magic

For a moment nobody moved or spoke. Then the
Unicorn exclaimed, "That's Hoppy's voice!" and
started off at a gallop towards the wood. Albert and
Tony raced after him as fast as they could, though in
Albert's case that wasn't very fast owing to his short,
stumpy legs.

"You—go—on," he gasped. "I'll come—as
soon—as I can."

Tony vanished into the trees and Albert toiled
after him, worried and fearful.

"What can it be?" he asked himself. "Someone
must be hurt or frightened. Is Hoppy one of the
Unicorn children? Oh dear, what can have happened?"

Still talking away he came to the trees and forced
a way along a narrow path which led through the
wood. The screams had stopped, but in the distance
he could hear the Unicorn talking very loud and
very fast in French. He sounded cross, but not
frightened and Albert took heart and stumped on as
fast as he could, pushing his way through the bushes
because the path was not wide enough for so large a
person as a dragon. Suddenly he heard Tony
laughing, and following the sound he came out into
a little clearing where the Unicorn stood, pawing
the ground and looking angrily at a very small

27

Unicorn who was so like him that it could only be his son.

When the baby Unicorn saw Albert he screamed again and took to his heels, disappearing from sight behind a little grassy hill.

The Unicorn turned to Albert and spoke rapidly in French. He sounded as if he was apologising but Albert couldn't understand a word he said. He looked at Tony, who only laughed again and shook his head.

"Forgive me, my dear old friend, but could you speak English?" implored Albert.

"I am so sorry. I am upset," said the Unicorn and it was plain to see that he was speaking the truth. "That silly little boy of mine! That he could be so rude and unmannerly! I do apologise, Albert, I do indeed."

"What for?" asked Albert. "What was wrong with the boy?"

"I don't know how to tell you," muttered the Unicorn, lowering his head until his splendid horn nearly touched the ground.

"I'll tell him," put in Tony. "Poor little Hoppy saw you through the trees, Albert, and you scared him stiff. Someone must have told him that if he was naughty the dragon would get him, so when he saw you—"

"But I wouldn't dream of—er—getting him," cried Albert.

"No, of course you wouldn't, but he doesn't know that. He must have a guilty conscience," chuckled Tony.

"The poor little fellow," said Albert, very upset. "I can't imagine why people are so often frightened

28

can't imagine."

"Oh Tony!" groaned the tiny Albert. "Whatever shall we do?"

Tony thought hard.

"Wishes always go in threes," he said. "That's one of the rules of magic. So far we've only had two, my lunch and your—er—"

"Don't rub it in," implored Albert, almost in tears.

"That leaves one wish," went on Tony. "We must find the Unicorn and persuade him to make you the right size again. And after this, Albert, to please me, just leave magic alone."

"Oh, I will," Albert promised in his tiny squeaky voice. "Let's go now, shall we? And would you be so very kind as to carry me, my dear friend? My legs will never get me through that enormous wood."

"It's only a thick belt of trees," said Tony. "Still, I suppose to a beetle-sized person it is a long way. Climb on to my hand, Albert, and hold tight."

"It's too humiliating," said poor Albert, clambering with difficulty from Tony's knee to his hand. "I can't think why I ever wanted to be small."

"You didn't want to frighten people," Tony reminded him. "But lots of people are frightened of insects. More people are frightened of earwigs than they are of dragons."

"Is that really so?" asked Albert in amazement. It didn't occur to him that this was only true because lots of people see earwigs but very few ever meet a dragon, and Tony thought it wiser not to point this out. Instead he set out for the other side of the little wood where he hoped to find the Unicorn again. But when he reached the other side with Albert clinging anxiously to his thumb, the countryside was empty of all life, and although he shouted again and again until his voice echoed off the surrounding hills, no Unicorns came in sight.

"*Now* what do we do?" came Albert's tiny, despairing voice, and Tony said crossly:

"It's no good asking me. You got us into this mess so you'd better think of a way to get us out."

"But I'm not good at thinking," Albert reminded him. "Do try and keep your hand still, I nearly fell off the edge."

"There's someone coming!" said Tony suddenly, and out of the empty air there arrived a form, shadowy at first, then thickening and becoming more substantial until before them stood the figure of a magician, in a long robe and a tall pointed hat.

"That's someone else I've met before!" said Albert excitedly. "I really believe he may be able to help."

The Italian Dragon

"Good afternoon my little man," the Magician said pleasantly, and Tony said, "Oh, hullo—I mean good afternoon. Albert says he knows you."

"Albert?" asked the Magician looking puzzled. "Who is Albert? I see nobody here but yourself."

"Oh, I forgot," said Tony, and he held out his hand. "Here's Albert. He's a dragon, you know, but I'm afraid he's had a little accident."

"He has indeed," said the Magician gravely, peering at the tiny figure on Tony's hand. "Albert the Dragon! Yes, of course I remember meeting him in—Cornwall, I believe?"

"Yes, that's right," said Tony. "He's huge really. I expect you remember that too. But he made a wish and the Unicorn got it all wrong, and now we don't know what to do. We're on our way round the world, you see, me riding on Albert's back, so it really is rather awkward."

"Dear me," said the Magician, and a slow smile spread over his face. "Dear, deary me. Wishes can be awkward if you don't quite understand how to manage them."

"I only wished to be small because I frightened the Unicorn's little boy," protested Albert, but his voice was so tiny neither of the others heard what he said.

33

"The trouble is," said Tony, "the Unicorn has gone off somewhere so I can't ask him to let me wish Albert big again. I suppose *you* couldn't help, could you? I know magicians are awfully good at granting wishes."

"Well, I could, of course," said the Magician. He bent down and looked closely at poor Albert, perched uncomfortably on Tony's thumb. "Rather sweet, isn't he? I always thought the only thing against dragons was their size. Why not let him stay small and make a pet of him?"

"I couldn't do that!" exclaimed Tony. "Albert is my friend, not my pet!"

"Certainly not!" screamed Albert so loudly that the tiny, thin sound reached even the Magician's ears, and he laughed and said, "Then we'll have to see what we can do. Put him down, my boy."

"Mind you don't step on him," said Tony, setting Albert carefully down on the grass. "That's him, just by that daisy."

"Turn your back," said the Magician. "I don't like being watched when I do my magic."

Rather reluctantly Tony turned his back. He was bothered in case the magic didn't work and Albert got lost among the tall grasses, but he need not have been afraid. He heard a few strange, muttered words and then something pushed him violently in the back so that he fell sprawling onto his face.

"*Dreadfully* sorry!" came Albert's voice, his proper voice, no longer a squeak. "I caught you with my tail. You're not hurt are you, Tony old chap?"

Tony scrambled to his feet and turned round. There was dear old Albert, his proper size again and with all his scales shining and glittering in the sun. Of the Magician there was no sign.

"Oh Albert! It is nice to have you big again!" exclaimed Tony. "I say, where is *he*?"

"I've no idea," said Albert. "People in France are funny, aren't they? They keep disappearing in the oddest way. Well, they say travel broadens the mind and I suppose we must expect odd things to happen. I would like to have said thank you, though."

"I'm still here," said a voice. "You can't see me, but that doesn't matter. I can see you, and very nice you look. Well, I'm off now. I don't very much want

35

to meet the Unicorn. He might be cross with me for un-wishing your wish."

"I think we'll go too," said Tony. "I don't want to see the Unicorn either. I think it was mean of him to play a trick on you. Let's be off, Albert. We'll never get to Rome before dark if we don't hurry!"

"It's lovely to have you the right size again," said Tony as he climbed onto Albert's back.

"You don't consider I'm too big and clumsy?" Albert enquired anxiously.

"You're exactly right," said Tony and Albert heaved a great sigh of relief.

"Off we go then!" he said cheerfully, and spreading his powerful wings he took off from the meadow and soared into the blue sky.

They came to Rome just as the sun was setting and the whole beautiful city was bathed in a golden light.

"It looks very crowded," Albert remarked. "I really don't know about landing right in the middle, Tony. People might stare, and you know I really am rather shy."

"I know how you feel," said Tony. "We don't want to make ourselves into a public spectacle, do we?"

"Certainly not," said Albert.

"I'll tell you another thing. There's a big place in Rome where men fight lions. Gladiators, they're called. Suppose they wanted to fight you?"

"Why should they?" asked Albert in surprise. "I've never done them any harm."

"They do it for fun," Tony said.

"Well, it's not my idea of fun," Albert told him. "Let's fly on, Tony, and find a nice quiet spot in the country."

"There's someone coming!" said Tony in a low voice. "It's either a huge eagle or else—"

"Or else what?" asked Albert in rather a shaky voice.

"Or else a smallish dragon," said Tony. "Yes, it is! It's a small, green dragon and he's seen us. He's waving a claw!"

"I'll hover for a moment," said Albert, "and give him a chance to catch up. Do you suppose it's an Italian dragon, Tony?" But before Tony had time to answer the little green dragon had come up alongside and said, in a breathless, excited voice, "Welcome!"

"He speaks English," said Tony in great relief. "Hullo! This is Albert from Cornwall and I'm his friend, Tony. Who are you?"

The little dragon nodded and smiled and said "Welcome" again, followed by a long speech in Italian which sounded friendly.

"I think he only knows one word of English," said Tony. "He's telling us something but I've no idea what it is."

The little green dragon looked at them enquiringly. Albert shook his head and said, "No speak Italian," very loudly and clearly as Mr MacSporran had advised, but it wasn't a bit of good. The strange dragon clearly did not understand. However, he smiled in a friendly way, pointed southwards and flew off, making signs to Albert to follow.

"He's taking us somewhere," said Tony. "We'd better follow. He seems very friendly and nice."

The little green dragon flew on southwards for quite a long way until Albert's wings were growing

weary and night was settling over the land. The moon came up, huge and golden, and by its light they caught a glimpse of the sea far below. The sight of it was so familiar that both Albert and Tony immediately felt happy and at home.

The green dragon signalled that he was about to land, and Albert followed him down. They came to land on a beautiful little beach lapped by the quiet waters of a tideless sea.

"The Mediterranean," said Tony wisely. "I learnt about it in geography."

"I don't care what it's called," said Albert happily. "All I care about is that there seems to be plenty of my favourite seaweed. We couldn't have a nicer place to spend the night. What a very nice fellow that little green chap is! Why, where is he? He's gone!"

"He hasn't gone far," said Tony. "He's just over there, in that field. I think he's picking something. Now he's coming back."

The little green dragon landed on the beach beside them. In both claws he held huge bunches of the most delicious grapes which he put down carefully at Tony's feet. Then he flapped off again and returned with a bunch of fresh seaweed which he presented to Albert. He really was the most polite and helpful dragon Albert had ever met.

"If this is what foreigners are like all I can say is that I approve of them," said Albert, through a mouthful of seaweed. He smiled and bowed to the little dragon who smiled and bowed back.

"Very—good. Thank—you!" said Albert very loudly and clearly. The dragon blinked and put his claws over his ears.

"He's not deaf," said Tony, giggling. "He's Italian. He might just as well shout at us and expect us to understand."

"It's quite a problem, isn't it?" said Albert. "I wonder who he is." He pointed to himself and said, "Albert," and then to Tony. "Him Tony!"

The little dragon nodded understandingly, put a claw on his chest and said, "Giorgio."

"It's nice to know his name," said Albert. "I wish we could ask him the way to China, Tony."

"I *know* the way to China," said Tony a little bit crossly.

"Of course you do, my dear old friend," Albert assured him. "It's just that it would be nice to make quite sure we are facing the proper way."

"I'll ask him in the morning," promised Tony, but when they woke up after a good night's sleep the little green dragon had gone.

Camels and Dates

"Where to now?" asked Albert, flapping his wings to get them working smoothly before he took off.

"Well, I've been thinking," said Tony. "The shortest way to China is all overland and a lot of it is mountains which might be rather dangerous if we want to fly low, so what I thought is, let's go about half-way down Africa, seeing the lions on the way, and then turn off to the left and do the rest of the trip to China over the sea. We might stop off at a nice island on the way."

"You really are awfully good at geography," said Albert admiringly.

'I got a prize for it once," Tony said proudly.

"I'm sure you deserved it," said Albert. "I say, Tony, I wonder what has happened to that little green chap? If it comes to that I wonder why he turned up at all. It's a bit of a mystery, isn't it?"

"I'll tell you what I think," said Tony. "I think the Magician sent him, just to give us a helping hand, you know."

"Possibly!" exclaimed Albert. "What a very nice thought. I always liked that magician, and he certainly is very good at granting wishes."

"Time to get started," said Tony. "The sun's coming up and it's going to be hot."

"Ready when you are," said Albert. Tony picked

41

up the saddle bags, fastened them firmly around Albert's waist and climbed onto his back.

"Ready for lift off!" he said, and Albert rose into the warm, sunny sky.

"I'm getting much better at this," he said. "That was almost a vertical take-off. Which way now, Tony?"

"Straight ahead," said Tony. "Over the Mediterranean and then straight down Africa. I'll tell you when to turn off to the left."

Albert flew on steadily until the coast of Africa came in sight. It was very hot and they were both getting hungry and thirsty and wondering about breakfast when Tony leant forward and shouted in Albert's ear.

"Down there!" he yelled, pointing. "It's an oasis!"

"Goodness me!" said Albert in alarm. "Is it dangerous?"

"No, of course not," said Tony, laughing. "It's a water-hole with trees round it. People travelling across the desert stop there for meals. Let's go down."

"If you're sure it's safe—" said Albert cautiously, and Tony said, "Of course it's safe. We shall find date palms there. You like dates, don't you, Albert?"

"I don't know any," said Albert.

"Not *those* sort of dates!" said Tony. "You don't have to *know* this kind, you just eat them."

"Things are certainly very queer in foreign parts," said Albert. "I thought dates were what you remembered your birthday by, and things like that."

Tony didn't answer. He was peering down at the yellow, sandy desert, and presently he said:

"Camels, that's what they are! Look, Albert, camels!"

"Do we eat those too?" asked Albert, ready now to believe anything.

"No, of course not. Camels are large animals. The ship of the desert, they call them. I think they are going to the oasis too."

"I hope they won't mind us dropping in," said Albert nervously. "Perhaps it's their oasis. We don't want to do the wrong thing, Tony."

"They won't mind at all," said Tony positively. Albert wondered how he knew, but he kept his thoughts to himself and began the descent towards the distant glimmer of water. He was very thirsty and the water looked cool and delicious.

They landed at the oasis just as the little group of camels arrived, plodding over the hot, shifting sand with their large, plate-like feet. They looked at Albert and Tony with expressions of surprise and disdain, but said nothing.

"I hope we're not intruding," said Albert to the largest camel who seemed to be the leader. "We only want a drink of water and then we'll be on our way."

The camel looked at him down its long nose but did not speak.

"He doesn't understand English," said Tony impatiently. "Leave him alone, Albert. Look— those are date palms—I'll pick some for you, shall I? Be careful how you eat them, they've got a stone in the middle."

The largest camel spoke suddenly, and in English.

"Help yourselves," he said in rather a grudging way. "All that is mine is yours."

"That's extremely kind of you," said Albert, and the camel said, "From England, aren't you? We get a lot of English tourists here. That's how I picked up the language. My friends and I often oblige by taking parties to see the Pyramids and other interesting sights."

"How splendid of you," said Albert politely. "Are pyramids good to eat, like dates?"

The camel laughed scornfully and did not reply. Tony, very red in the face, nudged Albert sharply and whispered:

"Pyramids are huge mounds of stone. Don't give away how ignorant you are, *please* Albert!"

Poor Albert didn't know where to look. All the camels were regarding him scornfully, and now Tony was ashamed of his old friend. It was too much.

"I wish I'd never come," said Albert, tears in his eyes. "I'm just a stupid old dragon who knows nothing and I'd be better off at home." He had a sudden great longing for his quiet cave on the Cornish coast and the company of his dear Dragonettes.

"Let's go home," he said forlornly.

"Go home!" exclaimed Tony. "But we've only just started. Aren't you enjoying yourself, Albert?"

"Not very much at the moment," said Albert. Tony turned from the date palm where he had been picking the ripe dates and looked carefully at his old friend.

"What's the matter?" he asked.

"I'm stupid and ignorant," Albert muttered.

"You've just said so. And those camels despise me; you can see they do."

"Camels look at everyone as if they despise them," said Tony. "It's well known. I'm sorry I said you were ignorant, Albert. I spoke in haste. Actually there are lots of things you know that camels don't."

"Such as what?" cried Albert eagerly.

Tony thought hard, but not a single thing came to mind. Finally he said, "Oh, lots of things. Don't worry about it, Albert. It's better to be good than clever, everyone knows that."

Albert, somewhat comforted, allowed himself to be led down to the water-hole. It was cool and restful there, surrounded as it was by a thick belt of palms. The grass was fresh and green and he lay down thankfully, having drunk his fill, and munched the dates Tony had gathered. They tasted delicious, fresh and juicy, and he ate quite a lot. The camels had moved off now and they had the oasis all to themselves.

"I quite like Africa," he murmured sleepily. "But where are the lions?"

"Further down, in the jungle," said Tony. "Don't go to sleep, Albert. We ought to be getting on, we've a long way to go."

"Just forty winks," murmured Albert with his eyes shut, then he suddenly leapt to his feet exclaiming:

"Something's tickling me! Whatever is it? Oh, look Tony! Look! It's a tiny, tiny dragon!"

"It's a lizard," said Tony, laughing.

"But it's exactly like me if you looked at me through the wrong end of a telescope," said Albert, gazing in a fascinated way at the lizard. "Only it

46

hasn't any wings. Let's take it with us, Tony. The Dragonettes would love to have it for a pet."

"It wouldn't be happy in Cornwall," said Tony. "It would be cold, and besides it doesn't understand English. Leave it alone, Albert, there's a good chap."

"Oh, very well," said Albert. "But we will take back a lion cub, won't we, Tony? I can't go home empty-handed to those dear children."

"We'll see," Tony said cautiously. "If we don't get moving we'll never find the lions at all. They'll all have gone to bed by the time we arrive."

"You do hustle a chap," said Albert, but smiling to show that he wasn't really cross, and with Tony safely aboard he rose again into the hot, African sky.

The Lions

"Africa seems an awfully big place," said Albert as, hour after hour, he flapped his way southward. "It's much bigger than Cornwall."

"You don't know much about geography, do you?" said Tony in rather a superior way. "Cornwall is only a county, part of England. Africa is a *continent*. That's even bigger than a country. It's *huge*."

"I never pretended to know any geography," said Albert, quite snappishly for him. "I don't know very much about anything if it comes to that. You're the clever one, Mr know-all Tony!"

"Hey—we're not quarrelling, are we?" asked Tony in alarm.

"Yes we are. You keep rubbing it in how ignorant I am and I don't think it's very kind of you. Here I am, flying my wings off taking you on a lovely world tour, and all you do is tell me I'm a stupid old dragon. I wish I was home again, I really do!"

Tony was simply stunned. Never had dear, good-tempered old Albert spoken to him like that. He leant forward as far as he could and tried to see Albert's face, but all he could see was an enormous tear trickling slowly down Albert's scaly nose. Tony had never felt so awful in all his life.

"Albert, *dear* Albert!" he said in a choked voice.

"I'm terribly sorry—I didn't mean—I never thought—oh Albert, please let's be friends!"

Albert made no reply, but the tears rolled down even faster.

"Albert, please land," said Tony in a desperate voice. "I must talk to you, and how can I talk properly when I can't see your face? You—you aren't really crying, are you, Albert?"

"Certainly not," said Albert in a muffled voice. "Just a little dust in my eye, that's all. What do you want to talk about, Tony? Geography?"

"*No!*" shouted Tony. "I want to say I'm sorry, Albert. I didn't mean to hurt your feelings. Please go down and let's have a rest. It's so hot, I believe the sun is going to our heads."

"Hold tight then," said Albert. "I'm going into a glide."

Tony held tight and said no more until Albert, after a long, slow glide, came to rest in the shade of some very strange, unfamiliar trees. Close at hand the jungle crowded in and the air was full of bird cries and the chattering of monkeys.

Tony climbed off Albert's back and walked round until they stood face to face. What he saw made him feel really ashamed of himself for having even mentioned geography. Poor old Albert's face was all puckered up and his eyes were quite red and puffy.

"Oh Albert!" he said in broken tones. "I really am sorry. Please forgive me. I wouldn't have hurt your feelings for the world."

"Nothing to forgive, my dear fellow," said Albert gruffly. "Let's forget all about it, shall we? Bother this dust, it's making my eyes water."

"Mine too," said Tony, and then they both burst

49

out laughing and everything was all right again.

"It's high time we stopped for a rest," said Albert, stretching out at ease on the grass. "This is rather a nice place, Tony. Not in the least like Cornwall, but nice in its own way."

"The monkeys seem to like it," observed Tony, lying on his back and gazing up into the trees. "That looks like some sort of fruit they're eating. I wish they'd throw some down. I'm hungry."

"Ask them," said Albert lazily.

"I don't speak monkey," said Tony. "It's a funny sort of language, isn't it? Nothing but chatter-chatter-chatter."

"All the same, they might understand you if you talked to them," Albert said. "I mean to say, you look rather like them. So perhaps the language is much the same."

"*I* look like a monkey!" shouted Tony. "Well, thank you very much Albert."

"Have I said the wrong thing?" enquired Albert, opening one eye.

"How would you like to be told you looked like a monkey?" asked Tony indignantly.

"I shouldn't mind. I think they are rather handsome. And I very much admire the way they swing from branch to branch. Now, I couldn't begin to do that, Tony, and I don't believe you could either. Go on, talk to them. I dare you to!"

"Oh, very well," said Tony. He got up and went over to a large tree where a whole family of monkeys were sitting, eating some brightly coloured, delicious looking fruit. "Excuse me," he said. "Could you spare us some fruit? We've come a long way and we're awfully hungry and thirsty."

50

The monkeys stopped eating and looked at him and then at each other. Then the largest monkey said something in his queer, chattering language and immediately three smaller monkeys began gathering fruit and throwing it down to the ground. Albert gathered up a clawful and stuffed it in his mouth.

"Delicious!" he said with his mouth full. "Try some, Tony."

"He really did understand me," said Tony in surprise. "Thank you very much," he called and the monkeys all chattered in a friendly way before swinging off through the branches to settle in another tall tree.

"A very nice crowd," said Albert. "I like them much better than those stuck-up camels. I wonder if there are any African dragons? If so, I should very much like to meet them."

"I've never heard of any," said Tony, adding quickly in case Albert should think he was being superior again, "but of course I don't know very much about Africa."

"You know about lions though, don't you?" asked Albert.

"Well, I know lions live in Africa, that's all," said Tony.

"What are they like? Fairly small animals?" asked Albert hopefully.

"Oh no, they're quite large and very fierce," Tony told him. "They go about in groups, I think, and it's called a Pride of Lions."

"Dear me," said Albert. "I'm not sure I like the sound of that. Let's have a little sleep, Tony, just to refresh ourselves before we go to look for lions. I'd like to be at my best when we meet."

It is easy to go to sleep on a hot afternoon but not so easy to wake up again. The sun was going down when Albert, who had been lying on his back with his mouth open snoring a little, finally opened his eyes, yawned, stretched, and, rolling on to his side, looked across at Tony who was still fast asleep, curled up into a ball.

"Seems a shame to wake him," said Albert to himself. "All the same, we ought to get a move on if we want to get to lion country before dark."

He got to his feet, rather stiffly, and had a good shake. His beautiful green and blue scales shone and glittered in the setting sun. The monkeys stopped chattering and looked down at him admiringly, and various brightly plumaged birds felt quite envious and flew away in a bit of a huff. They were not used to seeing anyone more colourful than themselves.

When the birds had gone it was all very quiet and still. A small snake slithered silently over the grass and disappeared into the undergrowth and a lizard, sunning himself on a rock disappeared into a deep crack. Then suddenly one of the monkeys gave a cry of alarm and in an instant they had all vanished, leaping from tree to tree until they were out of sight.

"Now, I wonder what startled them," said Albert aloud, and as he spoke he heard a rustle in the bushes behind him. He turned around as quietly as he could, his heart beating rather fast and there, watching him silently from the middle of a thick clump of bushes he saw a magnificent tawny head with bright yellow eyes, tufted ears and a huge ruff around the neck.

"Good gracious me!" exclaimed Albert. "You must be—yes, I'm sure you are! Excuse me, sir, but are you a lion?"

The magnificent creature did not reply immediately, but he came slowly out of the bushes and strolled up to where Albert was standing. He looked Albert up and down, walked all round him and then said:

"Well! I've seen some queer animals in my time but never anything as queer as you. What are you— some sort of hippopotamus?"

Albert was so pleased to find that the lion—if that

was what he was—could speak English that he forgot to be offended at being mistaken for a hippopotamus. He smiled in a friendly way and said, "Quite a natural mistake I'm sure. But no, I'm a dragon."

"Oh, one of those," said the lion. "We don't see many of those around here."

"Well, we don't see many lions where I come from," retorted Albert. "I'm on a world tour with my friend Tony. That's him, asleep over there. I say, how do you happen to speak English?"

"Picked it up over the years from the Game Wardens," said the lion carelessly. "They're the chaps who see we don't get hunted, you know. This is a National Park."

"Oh, is that what it is?" said Albert. "I thought it was the jungle."

"So it is," said the lion. Albert felt confused, but didn't want to appear ignorant so he only said, "Yes, I see. Well, it's very nice, whatever you call it. I say, do you mind if I just wake Tony up? I wouldn't want him to miss meeting you. If I may say so, it is an honour to be talking to you. I understand that you are known as the King of the Jungle?"

"That's right," said the lion. "I suppose you aren't King of anything in particular, are you?"

"He's King of the Cornish Dragons," said a voice behind them and Albert swung round to see Tony, wide awake and rather red in the face, with his hair tousled and his clothes covered in dried grass.

"My friend Albert is just as important in his own country as you are here," went on Tony, and Albert felt a warm glow of gratitude that his old friend should stand up for him so staunchly.

"Is that really so?" asked the lion in an unbelieving sort of voice. "And what are you?" He looked scornfully at Tony's untidy hair and rather grubby clothes. "Are you King of anything or just somebody's lunch?"

"Whatever do you mean?" cried Albert. "Somebody's *lunch*? You can't mean—"

"Take no notice of grouchy old Leo," came a new voice from the bushes, and out strolled a beautiful young lioness followed by three chubby cubs. The lioness smiled kindly at Albert and Tony and said, "Welcome to Africa. I hope Leo hasn't been rude to you. He's in a bad temper because the cubs woke him up when he was having his afternoon nap. I told them to leave him alone but there, cubs will be cubs."

The three cubs giggled and rushed up a tree where they lay along a stout branch, their tails hanging down. A good deal of staring and whispering went on, and it was easy to see that they thought Albert was a great joke.

"I've got children of my own," said Albert good-naturedly. "Adopted children, that is. And this is my very dear friend, Tony." He looked a little nervously at Leo as he spoke. He didn't at all like the idea of Tony being regarded as anybody's lunch.

"He's a boy, isn't he?" said the lioness looking at Tony kindly. "We often see them around here but they are always black. A pink and white one makes a nice change."

After that no one quite knew what to do next. The cubs came down from the tree and sat in a semi-circle staring at Albert and trying not to laugh. Albert got more and more embarrassed and Tony was obviously boiling with rage. Leo yawned and licked his paws. At last Albert said, "I really think we should be going now. It's been so nice meeting you, but we've a long way to travel before dark."

"Where are you off to now?" asked the lioness

politely, and Albert said, "China. But we're going over the sea."

"Turn left when you come to the next big river," said Leo. "That will take you to the Indian Ocean and I dare say you could stop off at one of the islands for the night."

"Mind the whales!" said one of the cubs and all three exploded into giggles. Albert couldn't see the joke but he laughed politely all the same.

"*Well!*" said Tony when they were airborne again. "I don't think much of lions. That Leo is simply a huge, conceited cat and the cubs have no manners at all."

"I thought Mrs Leo was rather nice," ventured Albert, but Tony only snorted. The idea of being regarded as somebody's lunch had really upset him and he said no more until they were well away from Africa and over the island-strewn sea.

Tropical Islands

"There seems to be a great deal of water in this part of the world," observed Albert as they left the coast of Africa behind them.

"Too much water if you ask me," said Tony. "It's time we stopped for the night, Albert, and where are we going to land? It will be dark quite soon and I don't fancy coming down into the sea by mistake."

"I'll fly low and we'll look out for one of those islands the lion talked about," said Albert. "I like islands. Remember our trip to the Isles of Scilly, Tony?"

"Tropical islands won't look in the least like that," said Tony. "There will be coral reefs and palm trees and turtles. Don't fly too low, Albert, or I'll get my feet wet."

They flew on just over the surface of the sea until quite suddenly it was night and the stars shone brilliantly out of a clear sky. The full moon made a path of gold over the ocean and Albert flew along it quite excited by the strangeness and beauty of it all.

"I can see something that looks like an island," called Tony. "It's not very big but I should think we could stop there for the night."

"Any palm trees?" asked Albert. "I've always understood that coconuts are very good to eat."

"I can't see any," Tony said. "It looks rather

bare, but I'm awfully tired, Albert, and I think we could just land there all right."

"Anything you say," Albert told him obligingly. "Where is this island of yours? Oh yes, I see. Hold tight then, and I'll go down."

The island was very small and rather wobbly. It was also quite bare and felt slippery underfoot. Tony was just about to jump off Albert's back when his old friend held up a claw to stop him and said in a low voice:

"Tony, stop a moment. There is something very wrong about this island."

"Wrong?" said Tony, yawning. "What's wrong, Albert? It isn't very beautiful, but surely it will do just for tonight."

"I'll tell you what's wrong about it, Tony," Albert whispered. "It's breathing, that's what."

"Islands don't breathe," scoffed Tony.

"This one does," insisted Albert. "It's breathing in and out, and it smells of fish."

At that very moment the island gave a tremendous plunge which nearly shook them both into the sea, and a huge jet of water shot out of a blow-hole right in front of them. Then the island set off at a tremendous pace through the warm, tropical ocean!

"It's a whale!" yelled Tony. "The cubs told us to beware of whales, but I thought they were joking. Can you take off, Albert? Quick! He's going to submerge!"

There was no room on the plunging, slippery back for Albert to take a run. He just had to rise straight up into the air, and this, with a great effort, he managed to do. And only just in time. As he hovered, wobbling badly, the peculiar island disap-

peared altogether and only another great jet of water showed where it had gone down.

"If that's a tropical island I never want to see another," exclaimed Albert in a shaky voice.

"It wasn't an island, it was a whale," said Tony. "My fault, Albert. I must have been half asleep. But look—over there to the right, I can see trees, and the surf breaking on rocks. That's a real island. Let's get there as quickly as we can."

"You're quite sure you know the difference between a whale and an island?" asked Albert, still a bit shaky.

Tony heaved a sigh and tried not to sound impatient. "Trees don't grow on whales," he explained. "I know that for a fact."

"Very well then, we'll risk it," said Albert, and changed course for the distant glimpse of palms. He alighted on a warm, sandy beach just as the moon went in and true darkness fell, and both he and Tony were so exhausted that they went to sleep without bothering to explore or even look for anything to eat.

They slept long and soundly and were awakened by the screeching of birds in the coconut palms around them. And they awoke to a magic world of sun and sea and sparkling white sand. It was hot, so hot that they both made a bee-line for the water and sank up to their necks in the cool sea, so clear that it was like bathing in light. Thousands of brightly coloured fish darted and played around them, while away on the coral reef the waves broke like a frill of white lace.

"I call this absolutely delightful," said Albert contentedly. "I wonder if anybody lives here, Tony. If so, they are very lucky people."

"Turtles live here," said Tony, floating happily on his back. "There's a big one coming towards us now."

"I hope he understands English," said Albert. It seemed the turtle did not, but he gave a sort of welcoming bob, like a little bow, and waved a flipper as he went slowly past.

"Let's hope there aren't any savages," said Tony. "Still, I don't suppose they'd bother us. You're so big, Albert, they'd be afraid."

"There you go again!" exclaimed Albert. "You know I hate people to be afraid of me just because I'm big."

"Well, don't go wishing yourself small again," Tony implored him. "You never know who might be listening. Perhaps the turtles can grant wishes."

"Now you're teasing me," said Albert good-naturedly. "I'm not likely to wish myself small again. It was a horrid feeling. If I could have a wish it would be that there are no savages here. It is such a beautiful island that I would like us to have it all to ourselves."

"If I had a wish I'd wish for some breakfast," said Tony. "I'm getting hungrier and hungrier."

"Then let us go ashore and see what we can find to eat," suggested Albert, and they left the water and walked up the beach to the shade of the tall coconut palms. It was now so hot that Tony's clothes dried on him almost at once.

"I've heard turtle eggs are good to eat," said Tony. "They cover them with sand and leave them to hatch out. I dare say we could find some if we searched around."

"Tony, you astonish me," said Albert. "Those eggs would be somebody's *children*. How can you think of eating them?"

"Oh well, if that's the way you see it," said Tony rather grumpily, and Albert said:

"Yes, it is the way I see it. Have a coconut instead."

"Sure they aren't anyone's children?" enquired

Tony. Albert thought deeply.

"I don't see how they can be," he said. "I suppose you could say that the palm tree was their parent but it seems a bit far-fetched."

"I was only joking," Tony said hurriedly. "Goodness me, Albert, if you started thinking like that you'd never eat anything, and then where should we be?"

"Where indeed?" said Albert. He picked up a ripe coconut which was lying under the tree and crushed it in his strong claw. Coconut milk flowed out and disappeared into the sand.

"That's not the way to do it," said Tony. "You make a hole in the top and drink it out of the husk. I know, because there were coconut shies at the fair which Dad took us to last year. You threw wooden balls at coconuts and if you hit them they were yours. I won two."

"Find something to make a hole with then," said Albert. Tony found a sharp piece of coral and soon they were both drinking delicious coconut milk. After that Albert made a very good meal of an unfamiliar but very tasty little bush while Tony ate a kind of fruit which the birds were feasting upon.

"If the birds eat it you know it's not poisonous," he told Albert, who said admiringly, "What a lot you know about islands."

"It's just common sense," said Tony. "I'd like to catch some fish but I suppose you'd say they were all somebody's children."

"Well, they are, aren't they?" said Albert simply.

The island was so beautiful that they stayed there all day, bathing and eating and just sleeping in the shade of the palms. By the time they began to feel they ought to fly on it was so late that darkness came down while they were still gathering fruit to take with them, so they resolved to spend a second night there before continuing on their way. They each had a nightcap of coconut milk and settled themselves to sleep on the sand, still warm from the day's heat. The sun went in, the moon and the stars came out and they fell asleep, lulled by the gentle lapping of the waves on the shore.

Albert woke first, and he woke with a strong feeling that he was being watched.

Savages! he thought with a thumping heart, and sitting up cautiously he turned his head to look behind him. What he saw made him give a great start of surprise. Standing under the trees, regarding him with an amused smile was none other than the Magician, and by his side, crunching a coconut, was the little green dragon from Italy!

More Magic

"Goodness gracious me!" exclaimed Albert. "How on earth did you get here? And Giorgio too! I didn't even know you were acquainted."

"We are old friends," said the Magician looking affectionately at the little green dragon. "It was I who sent him to look after you in Italy. It struck me that you were not really used to foreign travel and might be glad of a friendly guide."

"How extremely kind of you!" exclaimed Albert. "But do tell me how you come to be here?"

"You have not, perhaps, had very much to do with magic?" asked the Magician, seating himself at Albert's side. Albert shook his head. "A bit, here and there," he said. "I can't pretend to know a great deal about it. But before you explain, please let me wake Tony. He'll be as interested as I am to hear all about it."

Tony took some waking. He had to be shaken quite hard before he even opened one eye and growled, "Wasser marrer?"

"There is nothing the matter," Albert told him. "It just happens to be morning and some friends of ours have dropped in. Do wake up, Tony!"

Tony opened both eyes, stared at the Magician and his companion in silent astonishment and then said, "I don't believe it!"

"Neither did I," said Albert. "But it's true, though magical. Our friend is just about to explain. Are you properly awake now?"

"I think so, unless I'm dreaming," said Tony. "Do I really see the Magician, and is that Giorgio over there, eating coconuts?"

"You're not dreaming," the Magician told him. "It's all quite simple really. I have at home a magic mirror. Most magicians have one, you know. You only have to look in it and think of the friend you want to see and hey presto! there they are."

"That's useful," said Albert. "Unless, of course, the person happens to want to hide from you."

"Then they wouldn't be friends, would they?" said the Magician. "It only works with people who are truly friends. So, after you and Tony had been gone for some time I thought I would like to know how you were getting on, and I looked in my mirror and there you were, having a wonderful time on this lovely island. Ah ha! I said to myself, I wouldn't mind a bit of sunlight and warm sea, so I whistled up Giorgio and we came along."

Tony thought for a bit. Then he said, "How did you whistle up Giorgio? You were in France and he was in Italy. It must have been a very loud whistle."

"My dear boy," said the Magician. "I wouldn't be much good at magic if I couldn't manage a little thing like a whistle. Why even you can whistle, I should imagine."

"Yes, but not to be heard from France to Italy," said Tony.

"That is just the difference between us," the Magician told him. "Anyway, Giorgio joined me, we had another glance in the mirror to make sure

66

you were still here, and then we came along."

"How?" asked Tony. The Magician laughed. "You want to know all about everything, don't you?" he said. "By magic, of course. So much quicker and easier than flying. One day, perhaps, everyone will learn to do it."

"I doubt that," said Albert. "It must be a very *clever* thing to do. And some of us are not very quick-witted. Me, for instance."

"You underrate yourself," said the Magician kindly. "In a thousand years or so you may very well have picked up the trick."

"Has Giorgio picked up the trick?" asked Tony. "He doesn't look old enough, not if it takes a thousand years to learn."

"No, Giorgio came along under my magic," said the Magician. "By the way, it's rather awkward you and Giorgio speaking different languages. Shall I do a little spell so that you and Albert can understand what everybody says, no matter what they speak?"

"That would be absolutely splendid!" said Albert delightedly. "Can you really do that?"

"Nothing easier," said the Magician. "Go and find me five ripe coconuts, six very pretty shells and seven of those plum-like fruits that the birds are eating. Then we'll see what can be done."

Albert and Tony hurried to collect the things needed for the spell. Albert picked up the coconuts while Tony hunted along the beach for shells and Giorgio, with a grin on his face, offered to pick the plums. When everything was gathered together the Magician said, "Right. Here we go."

"Isn't this exciting?" murmured Albert in Tony's ear.

The Magician closed his eyes and muttered some very odd words. Then he pointed with his stick in the air, and stamped three times with his left foot. Then he opened his eyes and said, "All done!"

"But you haven't done anything with the fruit and the coconuts and the shells," said Tony.

"Oh those? No, I didn't really need those. I just thought they would make it more interesting," said the Magician. Giorgio burst into a fit of giggling and said, "*I* knew that! It was funny to see you hunting for them so solemnly!"

"I can understand what he's saying!" exclaimed Albert. Tony looked cross.

"So can I," he said. "And I don't think it's worth hearing. He's making fun of us, that's what."

"I didn't mean to," said Giorgio quickly. "Please don't be cross. It's lovely to be able to understand what you say. You see, the spell works for me too. Let's eat the coconuts and things shall we? Pity to waste them when you've been to so much trouble."

"I shall take the shells home for Tina," said Albert, gathering them up. "We don't get shells like this in Cornwall."

It was very amusing being able to understand what everybody said. Two turtles ambled up as they were eating the coconuts and stayed for some time talking in a slow, grumbling voice about a shark they had seen not far from the shore, and how noisy and tiresome the sea-birds were in the early morning, and other topics of interest to turtles. Then a troupe of small monkeys arrived and had to be told who everybody was and what they were doing on the island. Albert and Giorgio seemed to amuse

68

them very much, but they said they had seen plenty of things like Tony before, only the others had always been black.

"There must be savages here then," whispered Tony. "South Sea Islanders!"

"They come in boats," rumbled the largest turtle. "They live on another island and come here for coconuts. Sometimes they steal our eggs."

"What a shame," said Albert indignantly. "Why don't you move to another island where they can't find you?"

The turtle looked at him in astonishment.

"Move?" he said slowly. "Us, move?"

"Yes, why not?" said Albert.

"Turtles don't move," said the turtle gravely, and all the other turtles thrust out their long necks, waggled their heads and chimed in:

"Turtles don't move."

"Funny people," said Albert wonderingly to Tony. "You certainly meet all sorts on a world tour."

"Well, you haven't moved very much yourself until now, if it comes to that," said Tony. Albert considered.

"I moved from the top of the cliffs down to the beach," he said. "And I'll tell you this, Tony, if danger threatened the Dragonettes I'd move right away without loss of time. Dear me, how I miss those children. I do wonder what they are doing now."

"Do you really want to know?" asked the Magician. "Because if so, I can show you."

"More magic?" cried Albert eagerly.

"Very simple magic," said the Magician. "You could almost do it yourself. Go and look into that

69

rock pool where the water is clear and still. Look hard and concentrate on what you want to see. Yes, you too Tony, if you like."

Tony and Albert, full of excitement, went over to the rock pool and peered into its cool depths. Tiny fishes darted here and there and a sea anemone waved its deadly fronds hoping to catch a shrimp for its dinner. The sand at the bottom of the pool was silver-white.

"I can only see fish," complained Albert impatiently.

"Wait," said the Magician. "Watch and wait."

Tony and Albert watched and waited and presently the pool turned milky so that the fish could no longer be seen. Then it cleared, and there, before their eyes, was the beach in Cornwall with gulls mewing in the sky above and Alberto and Albertina just coming out of the cave accompanied by Mary Ann! They hurried over the sand and rushed, yelling with delight, into the little waves that fringed the shore where they screamed and splashed and ducked one another, shouting to Mary Ann who could not swim and was bobbing up and down in the shallows.

"Oh, bless them!" said Albert, his eyes full of tears. "How happy they look, and how well! Dear Mary Ann is obviously taking great care of them. I really believe Berto has grown since we left."

"Mary Ann seems to be managing them all right," said Tony. "That's a relief."

"I knew she would, the dear girl," said Albert. "Oh, whatever is Berto up to now? Look, Tony, he's caught a crab and he's trying to put it down Mary Ann's neck, the naughty boy!" Albert was so agitated that he leant forward as if to stop Berto in his wicked plan.

"Hey! Look out!" shouted Tony, but too late. Albert toppled head first into the pool, and by the time he had scrambled back on to the rocks the magic was over and the clear water showed nothing

but silver-white sand, little fishes and the hungry sea anemone, still hoping for its dinner.

"That was wonderful," said Albert. "Thank you very much."

"I think we ought to be getting on with our journey," said Tony. "We've still a long way to go."

"Are you making for China?" asked the Magician. "If so, Giorgio and I would rather like to go with you."

"But that would be lovely!" cried Albert. "Er— will you fly or go by magic?"

"I rather thought of going by magic," said the Magician. "It's quick, quiet, clean and far less trouble than any other mode of travel. May I offer you and Tony a lift?"

"I don't quite understand," said Albert and Tony broke in, "He's offering to 'magic' us to China. It sounds exciting. Do let's go, Albert."

"Yes indeed, certainly," agreed Albert. "What do we do?"

"*You* do nothing," said the Magician. "Stand close together and close your eyes or you might feel a little bit dizzy. Ready? Where's Giorgio? Oh, there he is. *Now!*"

Albert and Tony closed their eyes and Tony kept a hand on Albert's claw. They heard the Magician begin a queer little haunting chant, then there came a rush of air, then silence, broken after a few seconds by the sound of temple bells, chiming in a strange, unfamiliar cadence.

"Where are we?" cried Albert, half excited and half afraid, and the Magician's voice came from somewhere near at hand.

"Open your eyes. This is China."

China

Slowly Albert opened his eyes and looked around, and what he saw amazed him. They were in a city, and he had never been in a city before, being a country dragon born and bred, and the noise, the colour, the crowds of people confused him so much that he longed to be out of it all and back on his quiet, Cornish beach.

"Tony!" he cried. "Tony, where are you? Don't leave me for a second!"

"It's all right," came Tony's voice. "I'm here. Isn't this exciting, Albert?"

"Is it?" said Albert doubtfully. "It's a bit too much for me. I didn't know there were so many people in the whole world."

As he began to recover himself Albert saw that he and Tony were partly hidden from the crowd in a little side street which led off a large open square. Tall buildings decorated in bright colours rose up all around the square, in the midst of which something important seemed to be going on. Men in long blue robes with pigtails and little round hats were hurrying to and fro looking very busy and the hum of conversation mingled with the sound of bells which seemed to come from every point of the compass.

"Perhaps it's a market day," suggested Albert,

but Tony said, "I think it's some sort of a feast day. Where's that Magician? Perhaps he knows what is going on."

They both looked around for the Magician and Giorgio, but could see no sign of them. This was rather worrying because, as Albert said, when you are in a strange place among great hordes of strange people, a magician is a very useful sort of person to have around.

"Perhaps he's just made himself invisible," suggested Tony. "He may be quite close, only we can't see him."

"Speak to him then," said Albert nervously, and Tony said, "Hullo! Magician, are you there?"

No one answered, and they realized with sinking hearts that they were quite on their own.

"It's not fair," said Albert. "He brought us here and now he's abandoned us. It really is too bad. Even Giorgio would be better than nobody but he seems to have disappeared too."

"Well, what shall we do?" asked Tony. "We can't just stand here. We'd better go and look for them, don't you think?"

"How can you look for someone invisible?" said Albert crossly. "It's a silly trick, vanishing like that. I'd never do it myself and I don't think you would either, Tony."

"I wouldn't know how," said Tony. "Come on, let's go into the square and see what everyone is up to."

"Do you think it's safe?" asked Albert and Tony said, "They can't eat us, can they?"

"How do you know?" said Albert.

"Well, of course I know," said Tony. "I've

always understood the Chinese were very fond of dragons. I'll tell you one good thing, Albert. Thanks to the spell we shall be able to understand what they say."

"If the spell works here," said Albert and Tony nodded reassuringly. "It does," he said. "I've been listening and I heard someone say there was going to be a procession. I believe that's what they are all so busy about in the square. They're getting ready for the procession."

"Then I don't think we ought to butt in," said Albert, shrinking back into the shelter of the little street.

"Oh, come on," urged Tony. "What's the good of coming to China if we just hide ourselves? You can stay here if you like, Albert, but I'm going into the square."

He set off, and Albert hurried after him calling, "Wait for me, Tony! Don't go without me!"

The people in the square were all so busy that at first they didn't notice the newcomers, but a large dragon is not easily overlooked and it was only a moment or two before they were seen. The effect on the crowd was extraordinary. First everybody seemed struck dumb with amazement and then overwhelmed with joy and excitement. Somebody shouted, "He's here! The Great Dragon is here!" and the crowd closed in around Albert and Tony, shouting and cheering. Garlands of flowers were produced and flung round Albert's neck, and firecrackers began to explode all over the place, making Albert feel more nervous than ever.

"Hail, Great Dragon!" chanted the crowd and Albert said, "Thank you *so* much. Too kind of you.

75

But I'm not as great as all that, you know. I think you must be mistaking me for someone else."

"You are the Great Dragon from the West, brought here by magic?" enquired a very old man with an extra long pigtail and a moustache which drooped down on either side of his mouth. He wore a gorgeously embroidered robe and was obviously a person of importance.

"Well, I certainly come from the West," admitted Albert, "and, yes, I suppose I was brought here by magic, but—"

"Then you are he for whom we have been waiting," said the old man. Please take your place in the procession. We are late starting already. Is this boy your attendant? Then he had better come along too."

"But I'm not sure I want to be in a procession," protested Albert, but nobody was listening to him. A band struck up and made so much noise that he couldn't hear himself speak, so he shrugged his shoulders and decided that there was no harm in a procession, provided Tony went along too.

It was a splendid procession, at least half a mile long, with three bands and dozens of decorated floats drawn by horses. Albert and Tony marched somewhere about the middle, surrounded by men in brightly coloured robes who set off fireworks as they went. These made Albert very jumpy and the horses didn't seem to like them much either.

"I wonder where we're going?" Albert shouted to Tony, who stayed alongside although he had to run to keep up.

"I heard somebody mention the Great Wall," Tony shouted back. "You've heard of the Great

Wall of China, haven't you?"

"Never," said Albert. "Is it different from any other wall?"

"Higher and longer!" yelled Tony, his voice almost drowned by the chanting of the crowd.

"I've never been very interested in walls, I must confess," said Albert. "It hardly seems worth while to walk so far and with such a fuss just to see a wall."

The procession wound its way through the streets of the city and out into the countryside. The day was hot, and Albert, who was not used to walking, began to feel very footsore and weary. At last, when he realized he could hardly walk another step the procession stopped, the bands fell silent and the crowd, some of whom were as weary as he was, sank down thankfully on the soft grass.

"There's the Great Wall, just over there," said Tony pointing, but Albert couldn't be bothered to look. He lay down full length on the grass and found himself next to one of the horses, a splendid black beast as tall as Albert himself and dressed up to the nines in scarlet harness and gold bells. The horse turned his head and looked at Albert curiously.

"Hullo!" he said, and Albert was delighted to find he could understand him quite well. "You're an odd looking creature, aren't you? A dragon, I believe? We have a lot of artificial dragons here but it's the first time I've seen a real one."

"*Artificial* dragons?" asked Albert. "Whatever do you mean?"

"They make them out of paper and things," said the horse. He took a mouthful of grass and went on, "A lot of silly nonsense if you ask me, but then nobody does ask me. They must be pleased to have got a real dragon for once."

"They seemed to be expecting Albert," said Tony. "I wonder how they knew he was coming?"

"Oh, there's a prophecy," said the horse. "Something about, 'Out of the West the Great One comes.' I don't remember exactly how it goes, but everyone believes it. *I* never did, but it seems I was wrong for once, because here you are."

"But it may not be me they were expecting," protested Albert.

"There aren't likely to be two creatures of your sort," said the horse. "What did you say your name was? Albert? I don't recognise the name but I'm pretty sure you're the one."

"What is he supposed to do?" asked Tony.

"Don't ask me," said the horse indifferently and wandered off, cropping the grass as he went.

"There's going to be a picnic," said Tony hopefully and sure enough several girls hurried up carrying bowls of rice and vegetables and great baskets of fruit which they laid in front of Albert with bows and smiles. Then they all ran away, giggling.

"They seem to find me amusing," said Albert rather huffily, but Tony said, "I think they're only shy."

The picnic went on for ages. There was dancing, and a sort of play, and people sang and played strange musical instruments. It all seemed to be done to amuse and delight Albert and so, although rather bored, he tried hard to look as if he was enjoying every moment. Tony got so tired of it all that he finally fell asleep in the shadow of the Great

Wall, and it was because he was sleeping so soundly that he did not notice when the party was over that a great crowd of people surrounded Albert and began gently hustling him along the road by which they had come.

"I say—just a moment," said Albert to the people nearest him, "I've left my friend Tony behind. Could somebody please go and wake him up?" But nobody took any notice. Instead they began one of their queer, chanting songs and they hustled Albert along faster than before.

Oh goodness! thought Albert. Whatever shall I do now? I've not only lost Tony but I haven't seen the Magician or Giorgio for ages! The realization that he was all alone in this strange land nearly made him lose his nerve, and he shouted again, frantically. "Will you please *stop*!" But no one took any notice, they just kept on marching and chanting and Albert, trapped in the middle of the crowd, had no choice but to march with them. He was unused to so much walking and was getting very tired indeed when he saw, towering above him, a huge building all painted in gold and scarlet with a tall gateway leading into it through which the crowd were now pouring. The chanting stopped, and the air was full of the sound of bells. A great flock of white doves rose into the air above the gateway and their wings made a rushing sound as they soared into the sky.

"Where are we going?" cried Albert, but no one heard him because the bells and the birds drowned all other sound. The crowd surged through the gateway, Albert in their midst, and came to rest at last in a huge courtyard with, at the far end, a low stage beautifully decorated with flowers. To this stage Albert was guided and helped to mount the steps which led up to it. And then at last everyone was silent, looking up at him, and the bells stopped ringing one by one until they too were still.

"Whatever do they expect me to do now?" thought Albert in a panic. "Anyone would think I was a king the way they're looking at me. Oh I *do* wish Tony were here!"

But Tony was nowhere to be seen. Instead, another very grand old man in a beautiful robe approached him, bowed low, and said, "Welcome, oh Dragon from the West!"

"Thank you very much," said Albert. "It's very kind of you all, but I'd like to go home now. Will someone please find my friend Tony?"

"Go home?" said the grand old man smiling as if Albert had made a good joke. "Go home, honoured Dragon? But this *is* your home. We will keep you here, highly valued and greatly cherished for ever!"

It was a terrible moment for Albert! Stay there for ever! But what about Tony, what about the Dragonettes and Mary Ann, and his cosy cave on the Cornish coast? His whole being simply cried out for his simple life at home and the people he loved. Great tears rose in his eyes and poured down his face, and then, suddenly he heard a tiny voice somewhere close at hand.

"Stop crying," said the voice. "Don't be such a baby, Albert. I'm here to help you."

"Where are you?" whispered Albert and the tiny voice said:

"Look up the Mandarin's sleeve."

Albert had no idea what a Mandarin was, but the only person close to him was the very grandly

81

dressed old man so he peered cautiously up his wide sleeve and there was a tiny dog, the smallest Albert had ever seen. It had a beautiful, silky, tawny coat, two bright little eyes and a comical, squashed-in nose.

"Who are you?" whispered Albert, and the tiny dog said, "I'm the Mandarin's Sleeve Peke. I should have thought anyone would have known that. I've got a message for you from the Magician. Come a bit closer, I don't want to shout."

Albert edged nearer to the Mandarin who was talking earnestly to a friend and did not notice what was going on up his wide sleeve.

"That's better," said the little dog. "Now listen carefully Albert. This is what you have to do—"

The Rescue

Tony woke up slowly. He yawned, stretched and murmured, "I've had a good sleep, Albert. What about you?"

There was no reply.

"You're not still asleep are you, Albert?" said Tony. Silence greeted his words and he sat up and looked all around him in alarm. What he saw was so terrible that his heart beat like a drum, for the whole brightly coloured crowd had gone, the floats and the horses had gone and, worst of all, Albert had gone too!

"*Albert!*" yelled Tony and began to run back the way they had come. He was running so fast that he bumped into the Magician who suddenly made himself visible in the middle of the road.

"Oh, thank goodness you're here!" exclaimed Tony. "I've lost Albert! He'd never go off without me of his own accord. He's been kidnapped, that's what!"

"Calm down, my dear boy," said the Magician soothingly. "Albert has, in a sense, been kidnapped, but no harm will come to him. On the contrary, he is being treated as a very important person indeed."

"But Albert doesn't want to be important," protested Tony. "He won't like it at all. Where have they taken him to?"

"I have sent Giorgio to find that out," said the Magician. "And here he comes now."

"I can't see him," said Tony, staring into the sky.

"I made him invisible for safety reasons," said the Magician. "These Chinese are very fond of dragons and we don't want two of them kidnapped, do we?"

Tony privately thought that he would very much rather Giorgio was kidnapped than Albert, but he said nothing because he felt it would be rather rude. He heard the rush of wings and then the Magician muttered a few strange words and Giorgio suddenly became visible. He was panting slightly and seemed rather hot.

"Whew!" he exclaimed. "I've never flown so fast in my life. I knew you'd be worried, Tony, when you woke up and found Albert had gone."

"How do you know I went to sleep? You weren't there," said Tony.

Giorgio laughed. "Oh yes I was. We both were, only you couldn't see us. You don't think we'd let you out of our sight in a strange land?"

"That was decent of you," said Tony. "But I don't see why you had to be invisible. Why didn't you just come along in the ordinary way?"

"I had my reasons," said the Magician. "I saw an old enemy of mine in the crowd and I felt he was up to no good."

"He wouldn't hurt Albert, would he?" cried Tony, his face growing white at the thought.

"No, no, I don't think so for a minute," said the Magician. "But he might cast a spell on him to make him want to stay here for ever, and you wouldn't like that, would you?"

"Of course not," said Tony. "What would the Dragonettes do without him? But why should these people want Albert to stay for ever?"

"Ah, well you see," said the Magician. "They've always wanted a real dragon of their own and they have this prophecy (that's a sort of story handed down through the ages) that one day a splendid dragon would arrive by magic from the West, so naturally they think Albert is the one."

"Perhaps he is!" said Tony in despair.

"I hardly think so," said the Magician. "I've read the prophecy myself and there's something in it about the dragon being terribly wise and clever.

Now Albert is the dearest chap, but—wise and clever? I hardly think so, do you?"

"No I don't," said Tony with great relief. "He's not a bit clever. You don't think perhaps it's Giorgio they're after, do you?"

"He's not clever either," said the Magician. "Also, he's too small and the wrong colour. No, I'm afraid these people will have to wait a bit longer for their Wise Dragon from the West. The only bother is, suppose they don't realize how stu—er—not clever Albert is before they put the spell on him to make him want to stay for ever?"

"We mustn't let them!" shouted Tony. "We must rescue him at once. Why are we standing here?"

"Don't panic," said the Magician. "We've got a little time. Albert has been put on his guard. As long as he refrains from eating or drinking he will be safe. Most spells work through getting people to eat or drink. Of course sooner or later he will have to take nourishment and that is the danger, but he's been told to put it off as long as possible and that gives us time to make a plan."

Who told him?" asked Tony. "Giorgio?"

"Not directly," said the Magician. "I have a little friend who lives with the Mandarin—up his sleeve, as a matter of fact. Yes, he's a dog, a Sleeve Peke. Giorgio—invisible of course—managed to get a word with him, and he passed it on to Albert. I think that when we all leave here it might be as well to take Ping (that's his name) with us. I wouldn't like him to get into trouble if his part in this affair was ever found out."

"He could live with us at the farm!" said Tony. "We like dogs."

"We can settle that later," said the Magician. "The important thing at the moment is for me to think of a really powerful spell to get Albert and Ping safely away from the palace where Albert is being held."

"Can you do it?" asked Tony fearfully.

"Yes, I can do it all right," said the Magician. "But I shall need a few things which are not readily procurable. An auk's egg, for instance, would be a great help, and a whisker from a blue cat."

"But cats aren't blue," objected Tony.

"Persian cats are," said the Magician shortly. "Giorgio had better pop over to Persia."

"Any little thing I can do to help," said Giorgio obligingly.

"Then off you go," said the Magician. "Take care that the whisker comes from the *left* side of the face. And don't hurt the cat," he added as an after-thought.

Giorgio grinned and shot off into the sky.

"Anything I can do?" asked Tony.

"The best thing you can do is mingle with the crowd which has gathered outside the Palace and try to get in. The nearer you are to Albert the better because when I work my spell he'll be whisked off home and you don't want to be left behind, do you?"

"I should jolly well think not!" exclaimed Tony in dismay.

"Well, it's up to you," said the Magician. "I can't keep doing everything by magic, it's very tiring. You've got two strong legs, so use them."

"Yes, I will," said Tony. "What you want is for Albert and me and—er—Ping, to be close together when you work your spell. Right?"

"Right," said the Magician.

"And what happens then?" asked Tony.

"Then you go home. I think your shortest way would be over the North Pole. It will be cold but it won't last long. I'm going to use a method of travel which I learnt from the natives of Tibet. They've taught themselves to, as it were, *bounce* along with their feet only touching the ground every so often. Of course they don't do it by magic but you and Albert haven't time to learn it the hard way so my little spell will do the work for you. Mind you and Ping hold on tight to Albert because it's going to be a bumpy journey. Oh, and another thing. Try and make Albert really cross when you get to the Polar regions. Heat him up well—you know how hot dragons get when they're angry—and then you and Ping won't freeze."

"The only thing that makes Albert really cross is to suggest he eats meat," said Tony.

"Then suggest he makes a little snack out of Ping," said the Magician. "That ought to do the trick. Now, off you go."

It was much easier to get close to Albert than Tony had feared. He arrived at the Palace at tea-time and everyone was so busy eating and drinking, even the guards at the gate, that he had no difficulty in slipping past them and finding his way into the great courtyard where poor Albert was still sitting uneasily on the stage. He couldn't even enjoy a good tea like everyone else since Ping had impressed on him that he must refuse all food and drink because of the fear of spells. The idea of being put under a spell which would make him want to stay in China for ever was so dreadful that Albert was simply shaking with fright and he found no difficulty in refusing even the most delicious dishes which were being pressed upon him.

This refusal to eat was obviously making the people around him very cross. Tony, edging his way through the crowd, heard angry muttered remarks like, "Stupid dragon, what's the matter with him that he won't eat or drink?" and he heard one very grand person say to another that he was beginning to have doubts as to whether such a tiresome dragon was really the Great One they had been expecting from the West.

As Tony brushed past the two grand people a tiny voice said in his ear:

"Pick me up and hide me under your coat."

Tony looked all around but could see no one. The tiny voice spoke again.

"Hurry up, stupid!" it said. "I'm here, up his sleeve."

Tony looked and saw, peeping out from the wide sleeve of the grandest grand person, the funny little flat face of a Pekinese.

"Ping!" he exclaimed, and the little dog said crossly, "Do hush. And be quick. Really, boys are stupid!"

Tony put out his hands and Ping gave a little jump and landed in his arms. The Mandarin was talking hard and didn't notice a thing. Tony stuffed Ping inside his coat and wriggled his way through the crowd until he arrived, rather out of breath, at Albert's side.

"Albert!" he whispered, and Albert nearly fell off the stage in his joy and excitement at seeing his dear

Tony.

"You haven't had anything to eat or drink, have you?" enquired Tony anxiously.

"Nothing has passed my lips," Albert assured him solemnly.

"Just as well for you," said Ping. "My master is jolly good at magic and he'd thought up a really powerful spell to keep you here. By the way, if you're going home you might take me with you. I shan't be in favour here if it's ever discovered that it was I who told you not to eat or drink."

"The Magician said you'd better go with us," Tony told him. "If you like you can come and live with us on my father's farm. It isn't as grand as all this, but it's quite comfortable and we like dogs."

"Delighted, I'm sure," said Ping. "I really get a bit tired of living in the Mandarin's sleeve. It's no life for a dog."

"How long do you think it will be before the Magician gets us out of here?" asked Albert nervously.

"Well, he had to collect a few things for his spell," said Tony. "Giorgio has to go to Persia and back, but I don't suppose it will be long now."

"The sooner the better," murmured Ping. "I see the Mandarin approaching, and he looks very determined and rather cross."

The Mandarin came right up to Albert, followed by a small page carrying a bowl on a golden tray.

"Great Dragon!" said the Mandarin. "I beg—no, I *insist*—that you drink with me. It is the custom of the country." He picked up the bowl and took a sip.

"Now you," he said, holding out the bowl.

It was a dreadful moment. Poor Albert simply didn't know what to do. It seemed terribly rude to refuse, and yet he knew it would be fatal to drink.

"Don't touch it!" whispered Ping urgently from inside Tony's coat.

"Stand firm, Albert," Tony murmured in his ear.

"Take the bowl," commanded the Mandarin in such a terrible voice that in spite of himself Albert stretched out a trembling claw.

And then it happened! There was a rushing

sound like a great wind. All the people in the hall shrank back shouting in alarm and Albert, Tony and Ping were alone on the stage. They felt an upside-down, round and round sensation, the roof of the hall seemed to dissolve into mist and they were out of doors, racing over the countryside in great bounds, Tony clinging to one of Albert's back feet!

"Whoa—stop—help!" yelled Tony and Albert managed to stop just long enough for Tony to scramble on to his back and take a firm hold of the neckband which, luckily, Albert had never removed.

"Hold on tight!" gasped Ping, and then they were off again, crossing plains and mountains until Tony saw in the distance the dazzling whiteness and felt the biting cold of the Polar cap!

Home Again

The cold of the Polar regions was simply terrible. Albert was shivering so hard that he nearly threw Tony off his back and Tony's hands froze onto the band around Albert's neck. With chattering teeth Ping said, "Make him cross, Tony. Quick!"

Tony remembered what the Magician had said.

"A-A-Albert!" he managed to say through frozen lips.. "Wh-what about a little snack? Would you l-like to eat P-P-Ping?"

Albert was so surprised he almost stopped bouncing. Then his surprise turned to anger. Tony knew perfectly well that he wouldn't eat Ping. He was a vegetarian and wouldn't touch a chop, let alone one of his friends. The very idea! He began to get hot, fire and smoke burst from his nose and his whole body glowed, turning from green and blue to a beautiful red.

"All right, that's enough!" yelled Tony. "Look out, you're singeing my coat!"

"Don't cool him off too soon," begged Ping. "I'm just beginning to thaw out!"

But Albert was still sizzling with rage, and he bounced on over the snow and ice exclaiming at intervals, "The very idea! Upon my word! Tony ought to know me better!" and things of that kind.

Tony giggled, and warmed his hands on Albert's

glowing neck. When at last they were out of the
region of snow and ice he ventured to say:

"Sorry, Albert old chap, if you're upset. I only
meant it as a joke."

"A joke in poor taste," grumbled Albert, but
gradually he allowed himself to cool down.

A few more gigantic hops and they had crossed
the North Sea and England was in sight. It was a
most exciting moment. Ping put his head out of

Tony's coat and looked with interest at the green fields which lay ahead.

"Not bad," he said. "Not bad at all. I think I shall like England."

"You'll like Cornwall," Tony told him.

"Any Pekinese live there?" enquired Ping.

"I've never met any," Tony told him. "We've got sheep-dogs though, and there's Mr MacSporran of course."

"Who's he?" asked Ping. "What? A goat? Oh well, it takes all sorts to make a world."

It was nearly dusk when one last great bound brought them into Cornwall. Albert was so delighted to see it again that the tears came into his eyes.

"Foreign travel is all very well," he said, "but give me my own home. I'll never leave it again!"

They landed on Albert's own beach just as the sun was setting over the sea and the whole bay seemed to be turned to gold. Mary Ann and the Dragonettes were just sitting down to supper in the cave when they heard the sound of wings, and with one accord they exclaimed, "They're back!" and rushed out of the cave.

What a homecoming that was! Everyone kissed and hugged everyone else and everyone talked at once. Poor little Ping, still inside Tony's coat, nearly got squashed before Tony remembered to help him out and introduce him to Mary Ann, Alberto and Albertina. He and Mary Ann simply fell for each other straight away and she took charge of him as if he had been her little dog all his life. And in the midst of all the joy Albert suddenly looked round and saw the Magician and Giorgio standing near by, smiling kindly on the happy scene.

"Just dropped by to see you'd got home safely," said the Magician, and then he and Giorgio vanished from sight.

"A nice chap, but I've had enough magic to last me a lifetime!" said Albert.

"Me too," said Tony. "It's been a good trip though, hasn't it, Albert?"

"Yes, if you like trips," Albert agreed. "But for myself I'm just an old stick-in-the-mud, and I'm never going to leave my dear Cornwall again!"

And he never did.